D1451365

RayRay Paints a Self-Portrait

Written by Surayyah Fofana

Illustrated by Eliana Rodgers

Dedication

I want to dedicate the book to other "outsiders".
Kids who feel like they don't have a place to "belong"
or who don't fit into society's box.

Whether they are multiracial, neurodivergent,
or still grappling with who they are,
I want this book to serve as a reminder
that they can make space for themselves
and embrace being unconventional!

RayRay didn't just like art class.
She LOVED art class.

And she was sure today would be no different.
Today Mrs. Edelman had told them they would
be drawing pictures of themselves.

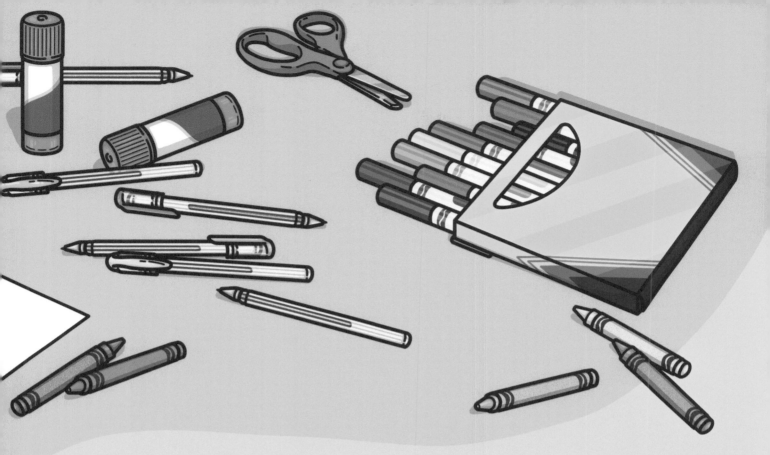

RayRay got out her glitter pens and began to sketch.
Soon, her drawing had a sparkly hot pink dress
and her favorite polka dot shoes.

RayRay was excited about her self-portrait.
It was colorful, fun, and a little silly, just like RayRay.
She finished drawing in her pink lips
and started on her hair.

Then she stopped.

RayRay looked up at the other self-portraits on the wall.
She looked around at all of her classmates.
And she looked back at her self-portrait.

RayRay's normally toothy grin turned upside down.
For the first time ever, she realized that
no one else had hair like hers.

All of a sudden, RayRay felt very alone.

RayRay was still staring at her self-portrait when the bell rang. Rolling it up, she shoved it in her bag. She would have to finish it at home.

On the bus, she slumped down next to her best friend Mari.

"Hey, Ray. What's wrong?" Mari asked,
her perfect curls bouncing up and down as she spoke.

RayRay just shook her head and looked away.
Why is my hair so different? she wondered.

At home, RayRay found her mom waiting in the kitchen with an afternoon snack: apples and honey.

As she crunched on her apples, RayRay inspected her Mom's hair closely. She noticed that it was long, blonde, and mostly straight. It reminded her of the yellow strands on top of a piece of corn.

That's not my hair!
RayRay thought.

Just then, RayRay's dad came into the kitchen
to make ataya, his favorite kind of tea.
It reminded him of Senegal, where he'd been born.

His hair was gathered into long, black dreadlocks that
reminded RayRay of snakes.

That's not my hair!
RayRay thought.

RayRay was disappointed.
She didn't have hair like either of her parents.
So who did she have hair like?
Where had her hair come from?

Then she remembered her sister.
Running upstairs, she found Sasha playing in her room.

Sasha's hair was gathered into two puffy pigtail buns
that reminded RayRay of the matzo balls
Grandpa always cooked on Jewish holidays.

That's not my hair, either!
RayRay thought, stomping her foot.

That night, RayRay and her family
went over to Grandpa's house for dinner.

When she arrived at Grandpa's house,
RayRay stared at his shiny bald head.

That's DEFINITELY not my hair! she laughed.

And Grandma's curls didn't look like her hair, either.

After dinner, RayRay felt energized to
keep looking for someone with hair like hers.

*If none of my family members in America have my hair,
maybe my aunts in Senegal will*, she thought.

As RayRay looked through a photo album
of all her African aunts, her sunny eyes
started to drizzle with tears.

"That's not my hair,
 and that's not my hair either! UGH!"
RayRay shouted.

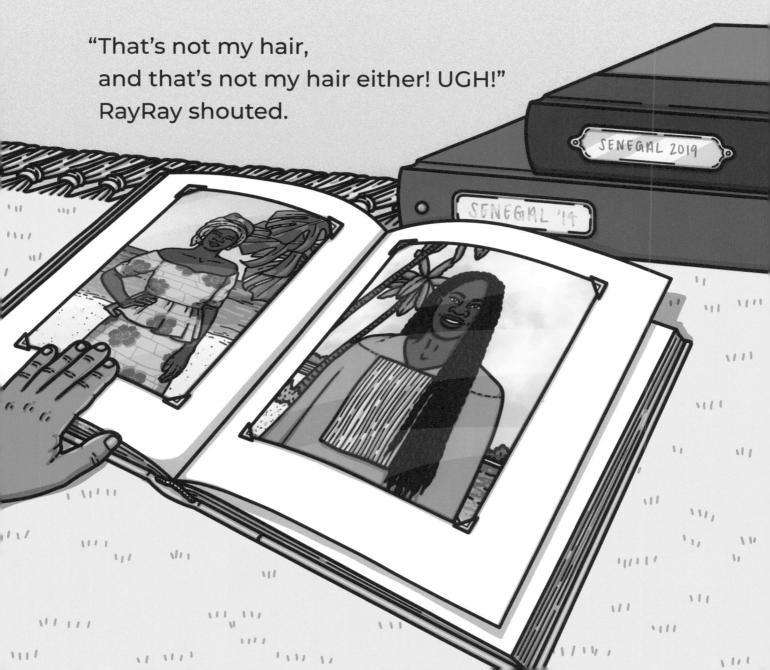

RayRay put away the albums
and went to sulk on Grandpa's couch.

How could she complete her self-portrait
if she couldn't figure out whose hair she had?

When Mom sat down next to her, RayRay groaned
and said, "I can't find anyone with the same hair as me.
I'm SO frustrated! How come my hair doesn't look like
anyone else's in our family?"

"Oh, sweetie," her mom said.
"Your hair is a mix of EVERYONE in our family.
 It doesn't have to look like my hair,
 Daddy's hair, or even your sister's!
 It is unique and beautiful, just like you!"

RayRay looked at everyone around her and realized that everyone had different hair.

She loved the way that Grandma's curls bounced when she talked.

And she loved the way that her Dad's dreadlocks fell neatly into his lap.

And—for the first time—she loved the way that her own hair was completely, absolutely, totally unlike anyone else's hair.

RayRay turned to her younger sister and said, "Your hair is unique and beautiful, too, just like you!"

The next day at school, RayRay finished her self-portrait and proudly presented it to her classmates.

RayRay said, "With my family's help, I realized that these self-portraits are all me, and these are all my hair!"

RayRay walked back to her seat, stopping on the way to give all of her classmates high-fives.

As she hung her self-portrait right next to the spot where Sasha would put hers next year, she thought to herself, *I can't wait to see our unique and beautiful self-portraits on the wall together!*

About the Author

Surayyah "RayRay" Fofana is a biracial activist, dancer, writer and high school student with a full head of phenomenally curly hair. *RayRay Paints a Self-Portrait* is her first ever children's book and it's based on her own experience as well as those experiences of families and children whose racial, ethnic and/or religious backgrounds mark them as unconventional in the eyes of the mainstream. Surayyah is interested in raising awareness around all things tied to race, culture, and diversity and creating a better more, inclusive world. She hopes this book can give readers an honest, warm and welcoming representation of a diverse home, much like the one she has the pleasure of growing up in.

Lightning Source UK Ltd.
Milton Keynes UK
UKHW050617091121
393619UK00001B/1